Sshshshsssish!

This is a magic book

un livre magique

These are Tilly's favourite pictures of herself

Tom

These are Tom's favourite
pictures of himself

7

These are Tiny's favourite
pictures of himself

9

Donkey

These are Donkey's favourite pictures of himself

And who's this?

One day

Tom pulled the curtains down,

Tiny got toothpaste all over the mirror,

and Tilly spilt her orange juice.

"It's an accidents day!" said Tom.
"It's a mistakes day!" said Tiny.
"Oh là là là là!" said Tilly.

The Tots went out in the garden.
Tom took a bowl of carrots for Donkey.
Tiny took a bag of biscuits for a picnic in the woods.
Tilly looked for her ball.

Tiny dropped his biscuits all over the grass.
"Oh dear!" he said, "It's an accidents day."

The birds came to eat the biscuits.
Tiny birdwatched. "That's nice!" he said.

Tom trod in a puddle and dropped
Donkey's carrots.
"Oh dear!" he said, "It's an accidents day."

But Donkey didn't mind.

And Tom played boats.

Tilly fell in a hole.

"Oh là là!" she said,
"C'est le jour des accidents!"

Then she found her ball.

What a happy accidents day!

Banana Tiny!

Tiny sometimes does silly things.
That's when he's a Banana Tiny.

Can you see the mistakes Tiny is making?
Point to them and say **"Banana Tiny!"**

Tom's bathtime counting

1 Slippery soap

2 Shiny taps

3 Tot toothbrushes

4 Happy ducks

5 Clean fingernails

6 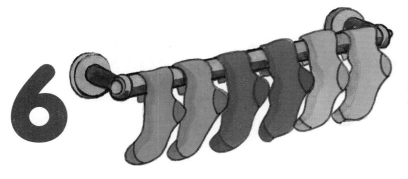 Socks to dry

7 Soft toilet rolls

8 Hairy legs

9 Wobbly bubbles

10 Peeping toes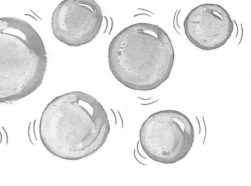

Digging holes
with Tilly

Tilly loves to dig in the garden with her spade.
You will need:

Something to dig with

a spoon

a spade

a stick

Somewhere to dig

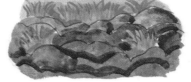

an earthy patch

a beach

Extra things

some water

a sieve

pots and pans

Tilly's word for hole

un trou

(say it like urn true)

Tilly likes to dig wide holes, narrow holes, deep holes and shallow holes.

Sometimes Tilly makes up stories while she is digging.

Tilly's not-true Story
The Underground Giant

Not-true stories are often the best. Tilly made up this not-true story while she was out in the garden digging a hole.

One day, Tilly was digging a hole. She felt something hard.

She uncovered a secret, underground door.
"Oh là là!" she said.

Inside was a secret staircase.
Tilly went down.
It was a long way down, and it was very dark.

"Hello!" said a big, deep, earthy voice.

It was an underground giant.

"What's it like outside?" he said, "I'm too big to fit through the door, you see."

"Comme il fait beau dehors," said Tilly, "le soleil brille et les oiseaux chantent et de temps en temps, il pleut."

"I wish I could go outside," said the giant, and he looked sad.

Tilly gave him a biscuit from her pocket to cheer him up.
It was only the size of a crumb to a giant, but he liked the taste of it very much.

"I only ever eat mud-and-water soup," he said, "for breakfast, dinner and tea."

The giant showed Tilly his saucepan full of muddy water.

"Bah!" said Tilly.
And then she had an idea.
She started to play a magic tune on her flute.

And as she played, lots of little plants started to grow out of the muddy saucepan.

Soon there was a whole garden growing out of the pan, with flowers and trees, and lettuces, peas, beans, tomatoes, and radishes.

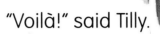

"Voilà!" said Tilly.

The underground giant was very happy. He tried a lettuce, and a tomato. He had never tasted anything like them.

"No more mud and water soup!" he said.

Tilly said goodbye to the underground giant.

She climbed back up the stairs and shut the door, but she didn't cover it up again, in case the giant wanted to peep.

Tom and Tiny wanted to know how she had got so muddy, so Tilly told them the story of the underground giant.

But she never found the secret door again. Never ever.

'Aaaaaaah'

'Pooooooh'

Tom's page of Smells

Tom likes smells best of all.
If he smells a nice smell he says "Aaaaaaah!"
If he smells a yukky smell he says "Pooooooooh!"
Point to these smells and say "**Aaaaaaah!**" or "**Pooooooooh!**"

I smell lovely with my talc on.

Tilly's word for smells

'les odeurs'

(say it like lays-or-derz)

Rainy days

It's raining today at the Tots house, but Tilly, Tom and Tiny don't mind.

Rain is falling from the sky,
Plip plop plip,
I don't know why.
Somewhere very very high,
There's a very big supply.

Tiny's rain bucket

Tiny keeps a bucket in the garden. When it rains, the bucket fills up with water so that Tiny can see how much rain there has been.

horrid lots of rain

lots of rain

more rain

widdly rain

tiddly rain

Tilly's word for rain

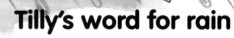

la pluie

(say it like laa plwee)

When it rains Donkey stays in his shed.
It is lovely and warm and dry inside.

Donkeys don't like rain. Their fur lets the
rain in.
Donkeys need somewhere warm and dry
to go when it rains.

But some animals don't mind the rain.
Horses, sheep and cows have special coats
to keep to the rain off.
When it rains, they can stay outside.

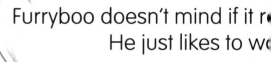

Furryboo doesn't mind if it r
He just likes to wa

Tiny likes to sit in the
window and watch the ra
Sometimes he sings quiet songs
If you sing a quiet song at the window
when it is raining, it makes a little misty cloud o
the glass. Tiny calls it his magic song cloud.
Sometimes it disappears straight away. Sometimes it stay
for a long time. Tiny thinks if it stays it must be a good son

Flowers like rain. It helps them grow.

Tom sometimes makes wormy sock friends when it's raining.

Fill a sock with toilet paper.
Screw up the end and tuck it up inside.
Stick on two paper eyes with sticky tape.
Now you have a wormy sock friend.
You can make more wormy sock friends, and they can have adventures.
Sometimes wormy sock friends want to drive a shoe car under the tables and chairs.

Sometimes wormy sock friends want to go to sleep.

Super fast!

Tilly's toilet paper game

You need:
Two empty toilet rolls.
Some squares of toilet paper, separated into two.
A table with a smooth top.

Play the game two at a time.

Sit at opposite sides of the table.
Put the squares of toilet paper in the middle.
Blow through the toilet roll.
Try to blow the toilet paper off the other side of the table.

Brilliant!

Sometimes you get covered in toilet paper.

Tom's boats

The rain makes puddles in the Tots garden.

Tom makes boats to float on them.

Float your boats on the sea.
Sail them away.

Anything that floats can be a boat.

margarine pot

plastic bottle top

paper

paper bag

yoghurt pot

sometimes boats sink

oh dear!

sometimes it's a good idea to have doors for passengers

Tom makes up stories about his boats.

Tom's not-true Story
Sailing on the sea

Tom made up this story while he was sailing his boats.

Tom went sailing on the sea.
"What a lovely place to be!"
Tom went sailing on the sea.

The sea swelled and swilled
and washed and sploshed.

And Tom's boat sank!

That's lucky!

"Hello!" said the seagulls, "Can we come to tea?"

Oh dear. Too heavy!

That's lucky!

"A far away island!" said Tom.

"Mind my head!" said the whale.

Safely home.

Tots together

Tilly's magic words flower

1 un

bonjour
(say it like bon-shure)
Tilly says 'bonjour' to say hello

au revoir
(say it like or-vwar)
Tilly says 'au revoir' to say goodbye

j'ai une idée!
(say it like shay-oon-ee-day)
Tilly says 'j'ai une idée!' when she has an idea

Oh là là!
(say it like oo-la-laa)
Tilly says 'oh là là' when she is surprised

Tom

Tiny

banane
(say it like ban-nan)

saucisse
(say it like sos-seece)

chaussette
(say it like shor-set)

moi

livre
(say it like leev-re)

2 deux

3 trois

pomme
(say it like pom)

gâteau
(say it like gat-o)

Donkey

fleur   magique

Oh là là!

Tilly says "**Oh là là!**" when she is surprised.
If she is **very** surprised she says "**Oh là là là là!**"
If she is **very very very** surprised she says
"**Oooooh là là là là là là là là là!**"

Look at these surprises. What would Tilly say?

Tilly's word
for a surprise

une
surprise

(say it like
oon sur-preez)

Tom's hiding!

Tom is hiding somewhere
in the garden.
Help Tilly and Tiny find him.
Start at the front door

look in the place where the
birds are eating biscuits

look where the animals are
climbing trees

look by the yellow flowers

look in the place where Tilly
has been digging

Où est Tom?

(say it like oo-ay Tom?)

look in the place
where Donkey lives

look
where the
clean
socks are

37

One day

Furryboo had a very rumbly tummy.

It **rumbled** and **grumbled** and **mumbled**.

Furryboo decided to go for a sniffle and a snuffle to find something to eat.

There was nothing in the drawer.

There was nothing in the sink.

There wasn't even anything in the dustbin.

But on the table, there were lots of yum-yum-yummly things to eat… And the Tots were in the garden.

First Furryboo ate a sausage.

Then he ate a cherry tart.

Then he ate some jam, straight out of the jar.

Then he ate some crisps and half a banana.

Then he ate a strawberry chocolate.

Furryboo was very happy.

But inside Furryboo's tummy, the sausage, the cherry tart, the jam, the crisps, the banana and the strawberry chocolate were all mixed up.

Furryboo's tummy started to grumble.

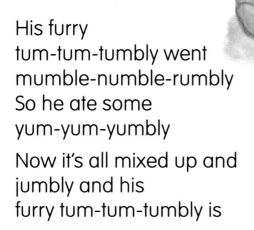

His furry
tum-tum-tumbly went
mumble-numble-rumbly
So he ate some
yum-yum-yumbly

Now it's all mixed up and
jumbly and his
furry tum-tum-tumbly is

trumble-drumble-grumbly!

Furryboo had to lie down and snoozle for the whole afternoon.

When he woke up, he felt better.

He went for a sniffle and a snuffle.

He found the biscuit tin, full of biscuits.

And do you know what he did?

He ate the whole lot!

Poor Furryboo's tummy.

Tiny's do-it-yourself Story tree

One day

Tilly · Tom · Tiny

found · sat on · ate · threw

a big book · a chair · a boiled egg · a football · a banana

in the woods · with three bears · at the table · and · and · out of the window

it flew up in the air and went · didn't feel very well · because

and read it · and turned it upside down · put salt and pepper on · to the moon · so went · he wanted to

to Donkey · and drew a face on it · and swallowed it · on · the roof · to bed

43

Time for bed

Night time comes
and it's time for bed.
Time to rest your sleepy head.
Close your eyes,
one two three.
I wonder what our dreams will be.

Maybe we'll dream about a magic rainy day window,
or about visiting the underground giant,
or about sailing away across the sea on a whale.

Or maybe we'll dream about
the magic secret house
where Tilly, Tom and Tiny live,
far away in the middle of a wood.

Goodnight house

Hold this page up to a light,
and watch the night-time come.